African Elephants

by Grace Hansen

Abdo Kids Jumbo is an Imprint of Abdo Kids
abdopublishing.com

abdopublishing.com

Published by Abdo Kids, a division of ABDO, P.O. Box 398166, Minneapolis, Minnesota 55439.
Copyright © 2019 by Abdo Consulting Group, Inc. International copyrights reserved in all countries. No part of this book may be reproduced in any form without written permission from the publisher.
Abdo Kids Jumbo™ is a trademark and logo of Abdo Kids.

052018

092018

Photo Credits: iStock, Shutterstock

Production Contributors: Teddy Borth, Jennie Forsberg, Grace Hansen

Design Contributors: Dorothy Toth, Laura Mitchell

Library of Congress Control Number: 2017960563

Publisher's Cataloging-in-Publication Data

Names: Hansen, Grace, author.

Title: African elephants / by Grace Hansen.

Description: Minneapolis, Minnesota : Abdo Kids, 2019. | Series: Super species | Includes glossary, index and online resources (page 24).

Identifiers: ISBN 9781532108211 (lib.bdg.) | ISBN 9781532109195 (ebook) | ISBN 9781532109683 (Read-to-me ebook)

Subjects: LCSH: African elephant--Juvenile literature. | Body size--Juvenile literature. | Animals--Size--Juvenile literature. | Animal behavior--Juvenile literature.

Classification: DDC 599.61096--dc23

Table of Contents

Biggest Animal on Land

African elephants are the largest elephant **species**. They are also the largest land animals!

African elephants can grow up to 13 feet (4.0 m) tall. That is taller than an NBA basketball hoop.

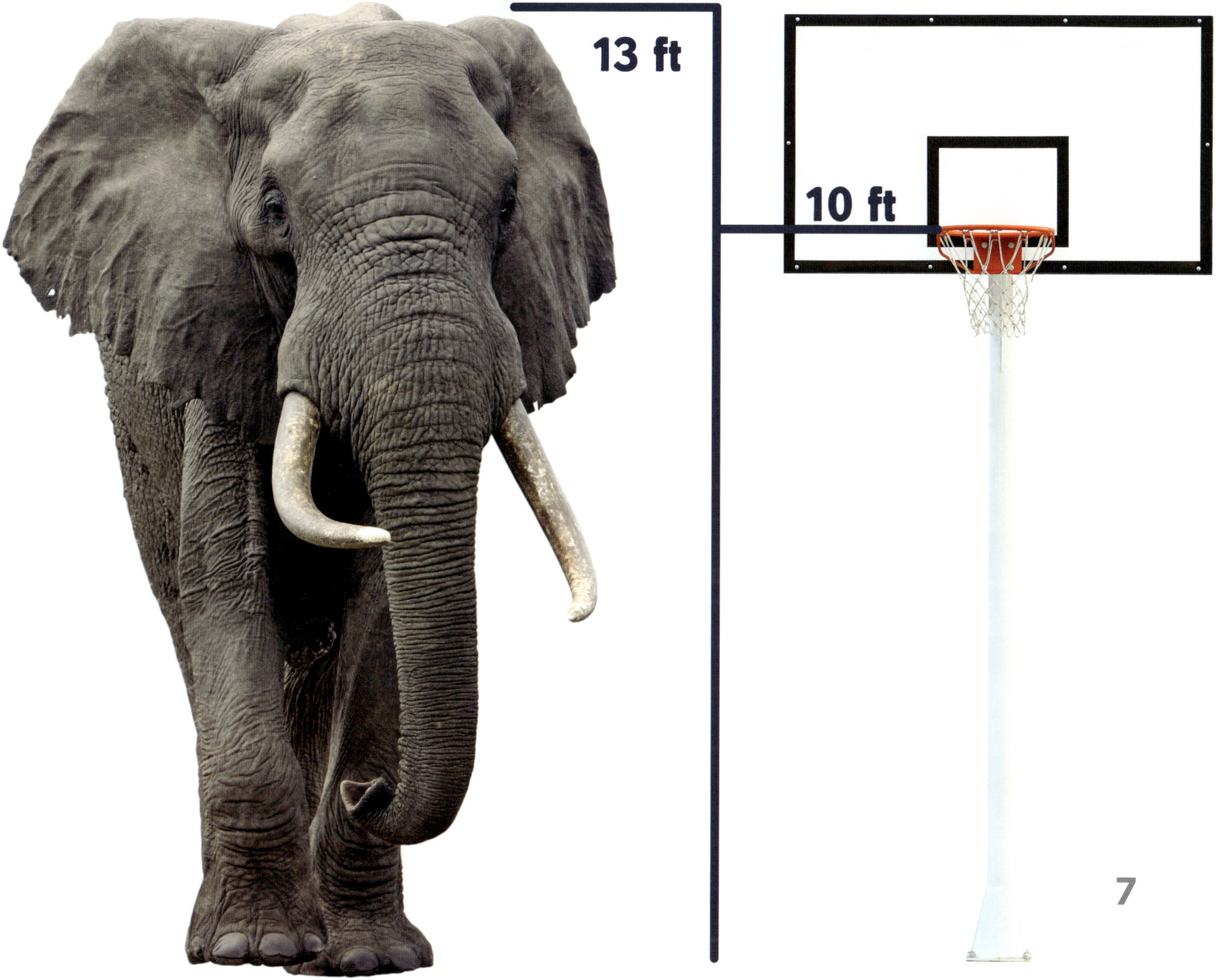

13 ft

African elephants can grow up to 24 feet (7.3 m) long. That is longer than a car!

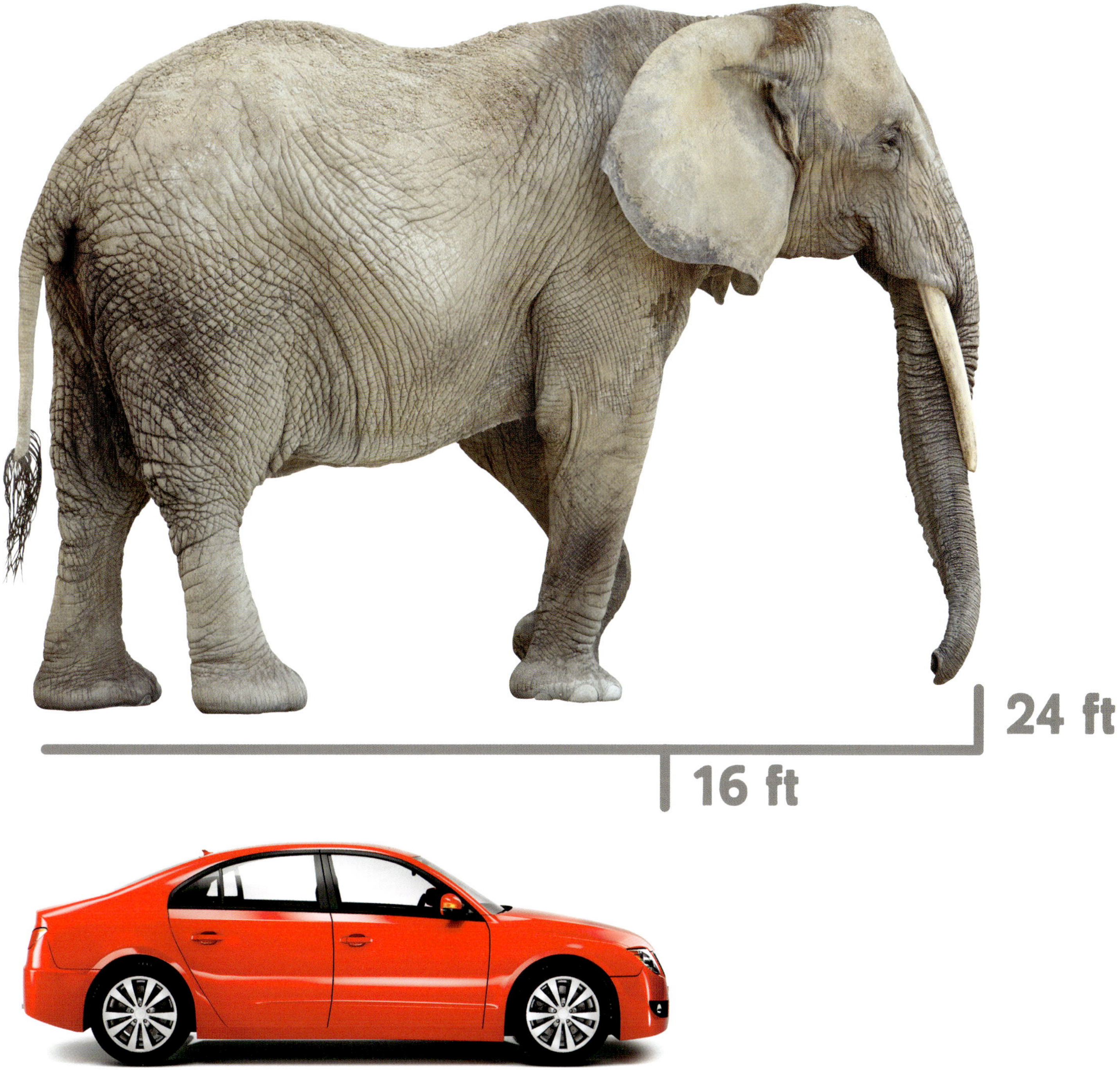

24 ft

An African elephant can weigh up to 14,000 pounds (6,350 kg). That is more than the weight of 33 male lions!

1

33

They have large ears. The African sun can be very hot. Their ears help them move heat away from their bodies.

African elephants have trunks. Their trunks can grow up to 7 feet (2.1 m) long! They use them to smell, breathe, drink, and make noise.

Food

They also use their trunks to grab and eat food. African elephants like to eat grasses, fruit, **bark**, and other plants.

They eat a lot! They have to eat at least 300 pounds (136 kg) of food each day.

Baby African Elephants

Female elephants give birth to one **calf** every two to four years. Calves are around 3 feet (0.9 m) tall. They already weigh 200 pounds (91 kg) at birth!

More Facts

- African Elephants are slightly larger than Asian elephants. And African bush elephants are larger than African forest elephants.

- Male and female African elephants have large tusks. They use their tusks to dig. Males use them to fight.

- An elephant's trunk has around 100,000 different muscles.

Glossary

bark – the covering of the woody stems, branches, and roots of plants.

calf – a baby elephant.

species – a group of living things that look alike and can have babies together.

Index

Visit **abdokids.com** and use this code to access crafts, games, videos, and more!